The pandemic of 2021 gave
myself and my talented son
James the unique opportunity to
spend time creatively together.

We created this book to help
educate the younger generations
about the importance of careful
recycling and product selection.

This book is dedicated to the hope
of a brighter future for all of the
creatures on our planet Earth.

This is the tale of Walter the whale,
Walter the whale and his plastic tail!

Walter the whale loved to swish through the sea,
with all of his pals in his whale pod family.

Each day a new adventure began,
the sun would come up and away Walter swam.

"Look at me!" said Walter to his pod family,
"Look at me splash
and make waves through the sea!"

"Come along Walter" said old Papa whale,
"We need to catch krill where the ocean's less pale".

The family set sail
to the waters less pale.
"I'm coming!" called Walter
to old Papa whale.

As Walter hurried his tail became caught!
"My tail is stuck fast but to what?" Walter thought.

An old fishing net was stuck tight to his tail,
but it was ok, Walter could still sail.
He rather liked his new novelty tail.

"Waaaaait Papa whale, I can still sail,
I can still sail with this funny net tail!".
Walter splashed and he dived
with his tail through the waves.

"I'm the magnificent Walter the whale,
look at my fancy and netty new tail!".

But, the more Walter sailed the more his tail filled
with bottles and plastic, Walter wasn't so thrilled.

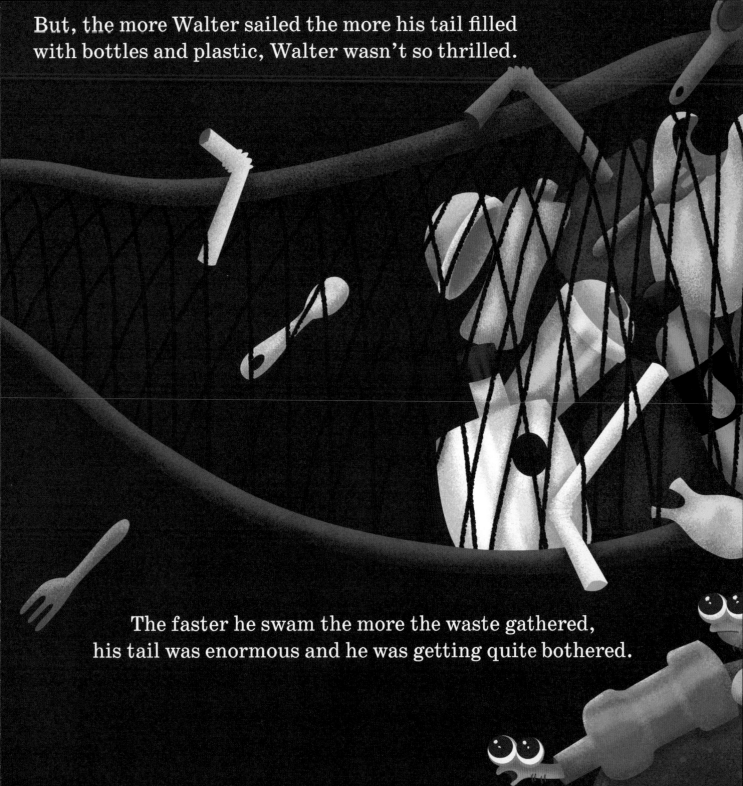

The faster he swam the more the waste gathered,
his tail was enormous and he was getting quite bothered.

Poor little Walter
could no longer dive,
all he could do
was bob along with the tide.

"Oh deary me!" whaled Walter the whale.
"I no longer like my huge plastic tail!".

The sun went down
and the day turned to night,
Walter exhausted
continued to fight.

He could no longer fight
and could no longer swim,
poor Walters fate
was looking quite grim.

Up in the distance Walter spotted a boat,
he tried to swim away but only managed to float.

Suddenly Walter heard a young voice shout,
"I see a whale with an enormous net tail!".

Out from the dark
Walter spotted a man,
a man and his son
and they both had a plan!

"Quick fetch our tools
and we'll set the whale free,
however did this much plastic
get into the sea?"

They carved the net carefully
and Walter slipped free
diving over the boat
and deep into the sea.

"Yippee!" cried Walter, "I'm now free to sail,
I can splash and dive and not be stuck to that tail!"

"Onwards I go, I'm now plastic free.
"I'm coming!" he called to his whale pod family.

"Be safe little whale,"
said the boy to his dad.
"We saved that poor whale,
I'm so very glad."

"The ocean is never a place for this waste,
it must be removed correctly with haste!".

They hooked up the net
filled with plastic and rubble
and towed it to land
where it could cause no more trouble.

They disposed of it safely
in the recycling bin,
to be turned into something
more useful again.

The next time you see someone dumping their plastic,
please tell them the story of Walter so tragic.

Tell them the story of Walter the whale,
Walter the whale and his plastic tail.

Our friends in the ocean deserve to be safe,
their home should never be a place for our waste.

Keep the beaches clean and the oceans clear
and whales like Walter will have nothing to fear.

We don't need a handful
of people doing zero
waste perfectly.

We need millions
of people doing it
imperfectly.

Keep the beaches clean and the oceans clear • and whales like Walter will have nothing to fear •

Printed in Great Britain
by Amazon